I Can

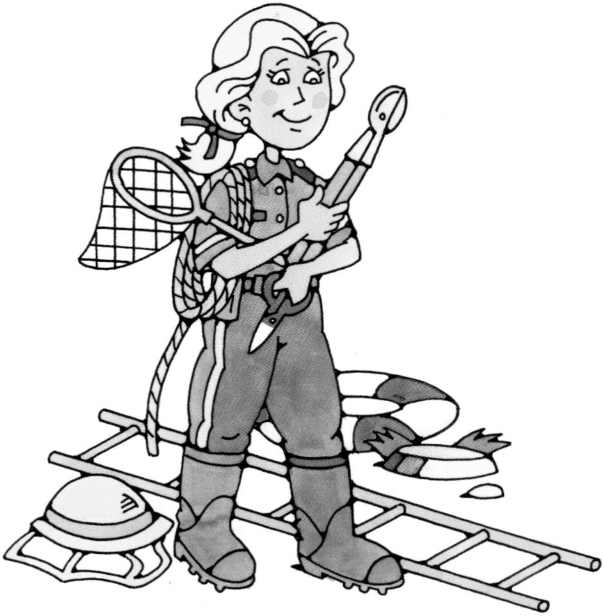

Illustrated by Kelvin Hawley

Rigby

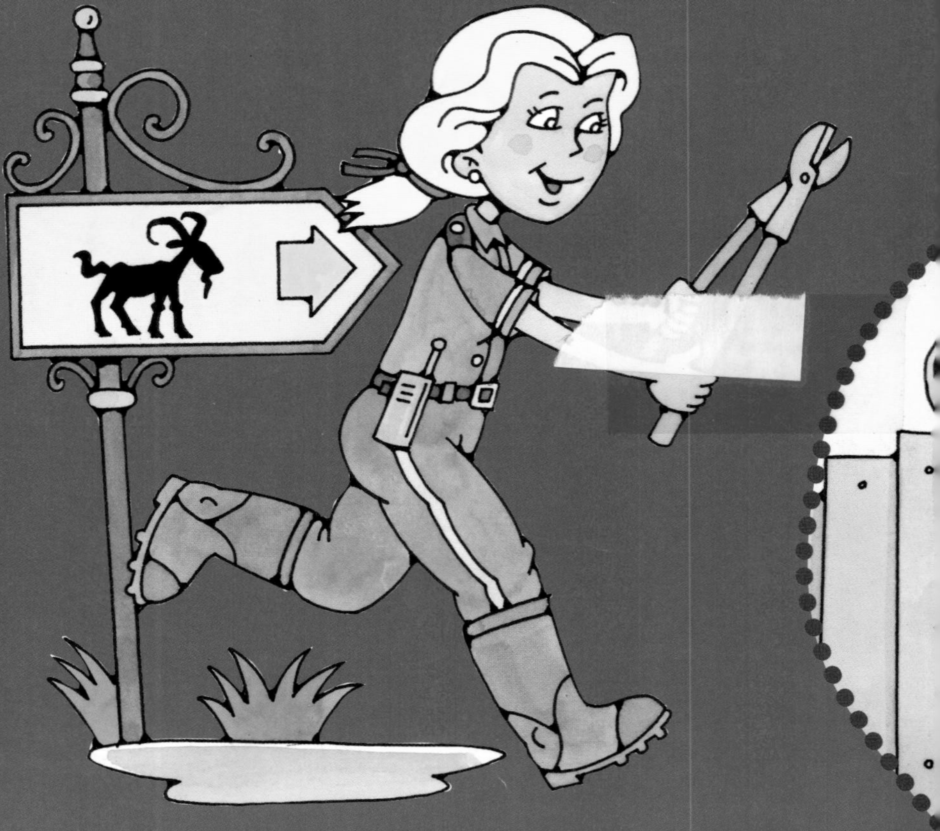

I can get the goat.

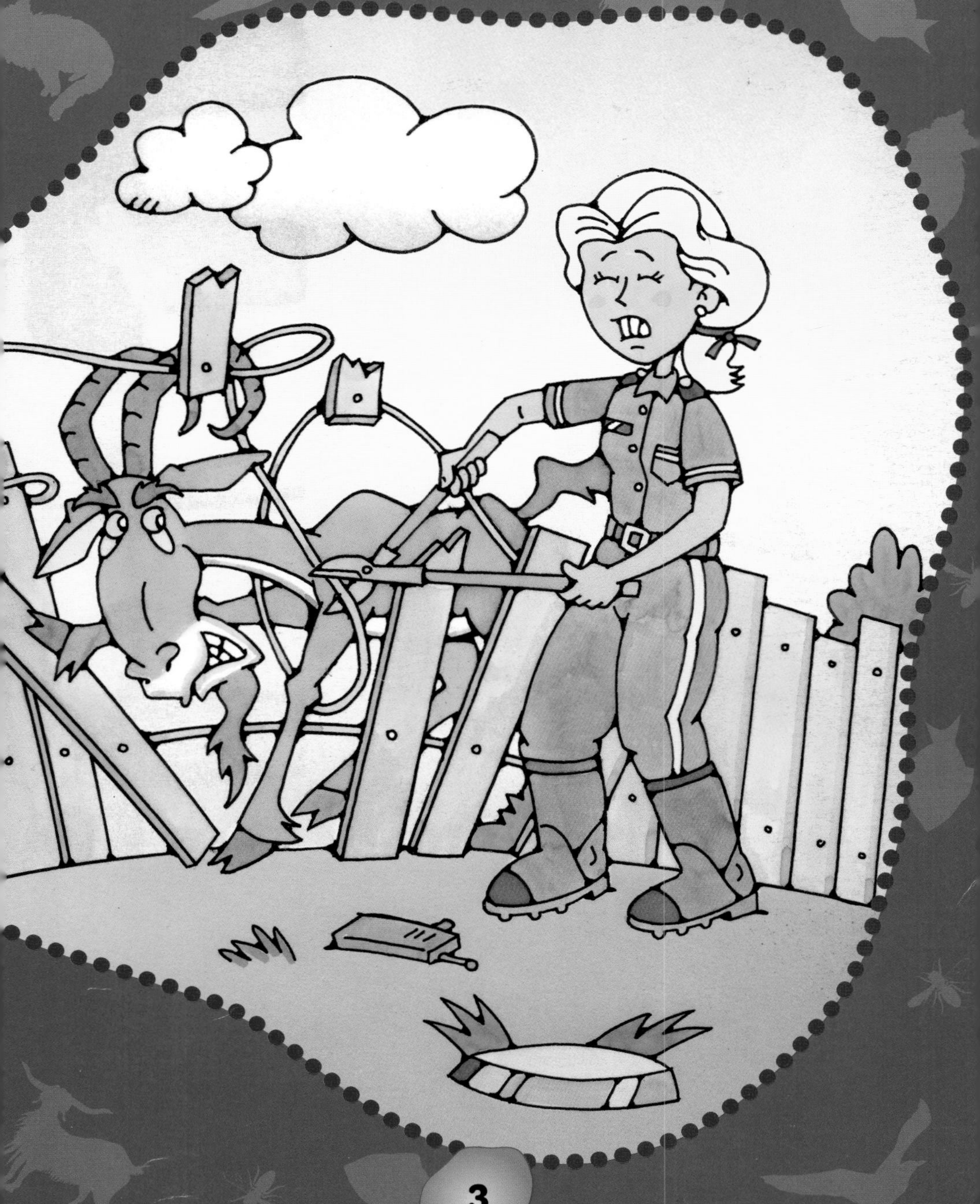

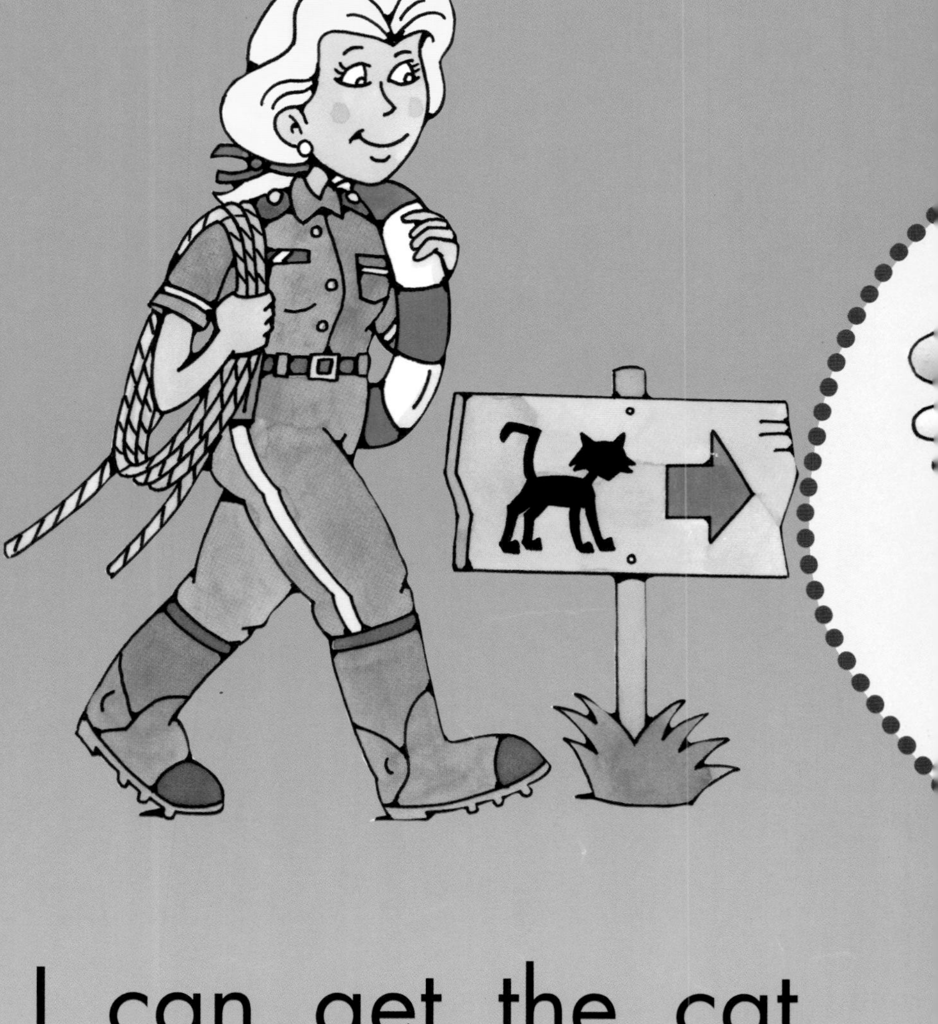

I can get the cat.

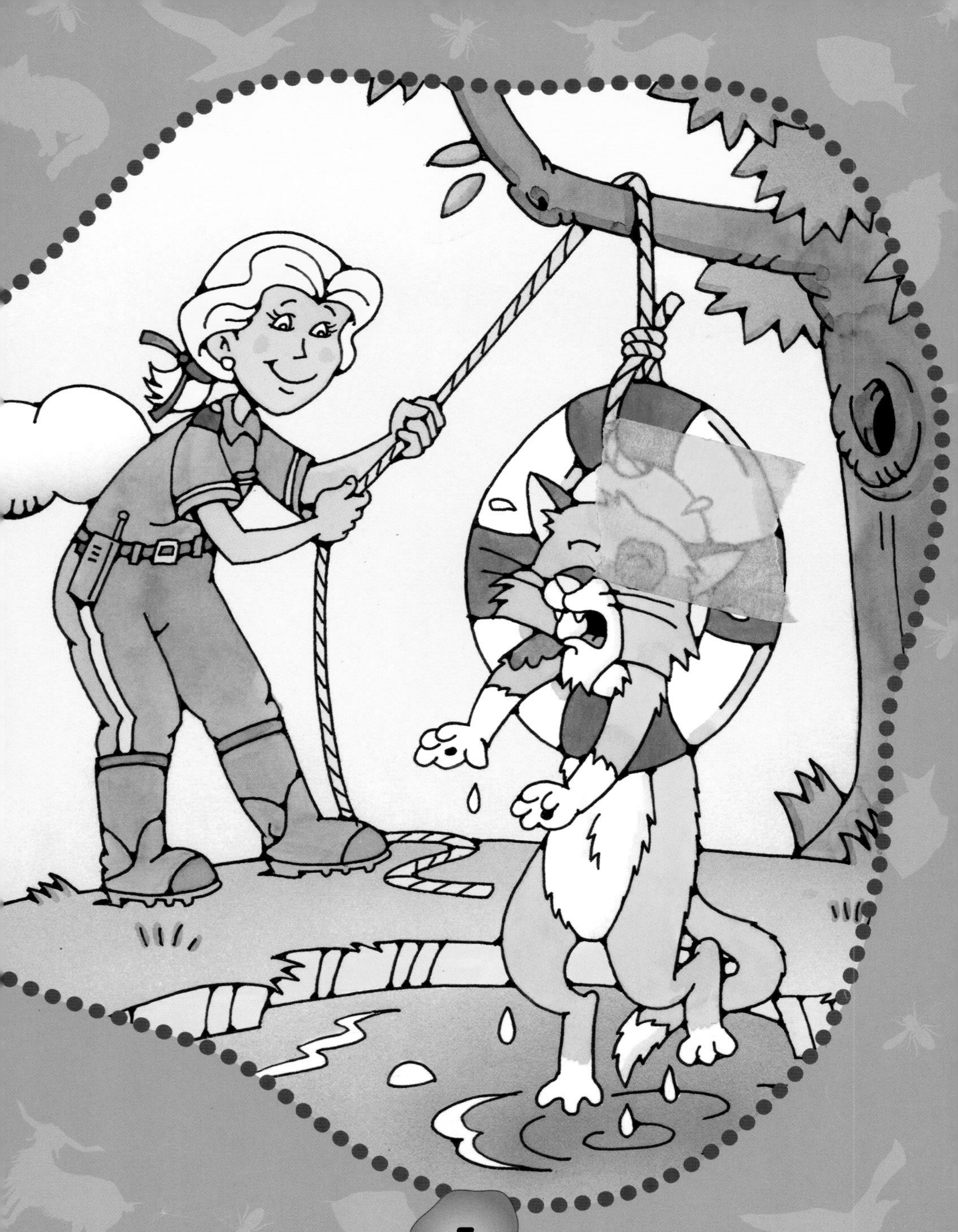

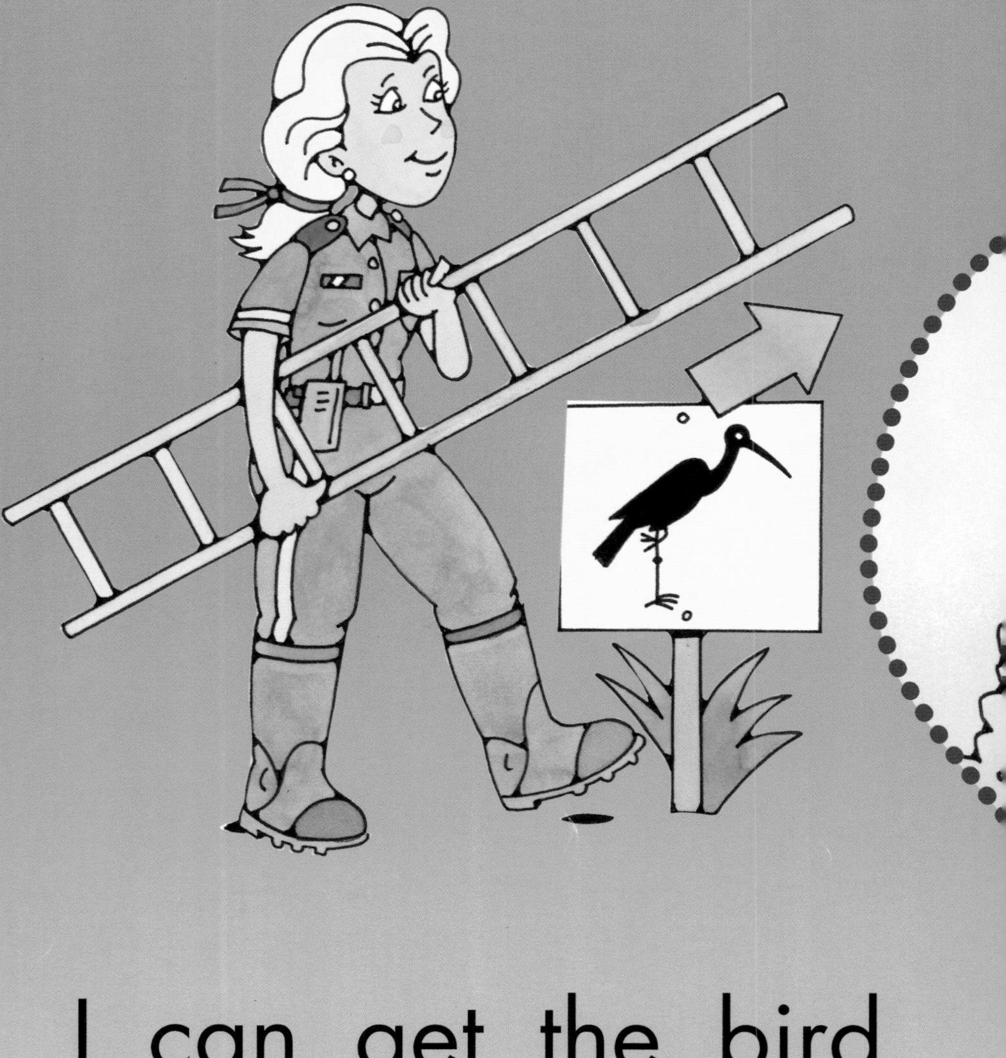

I can get the bird.

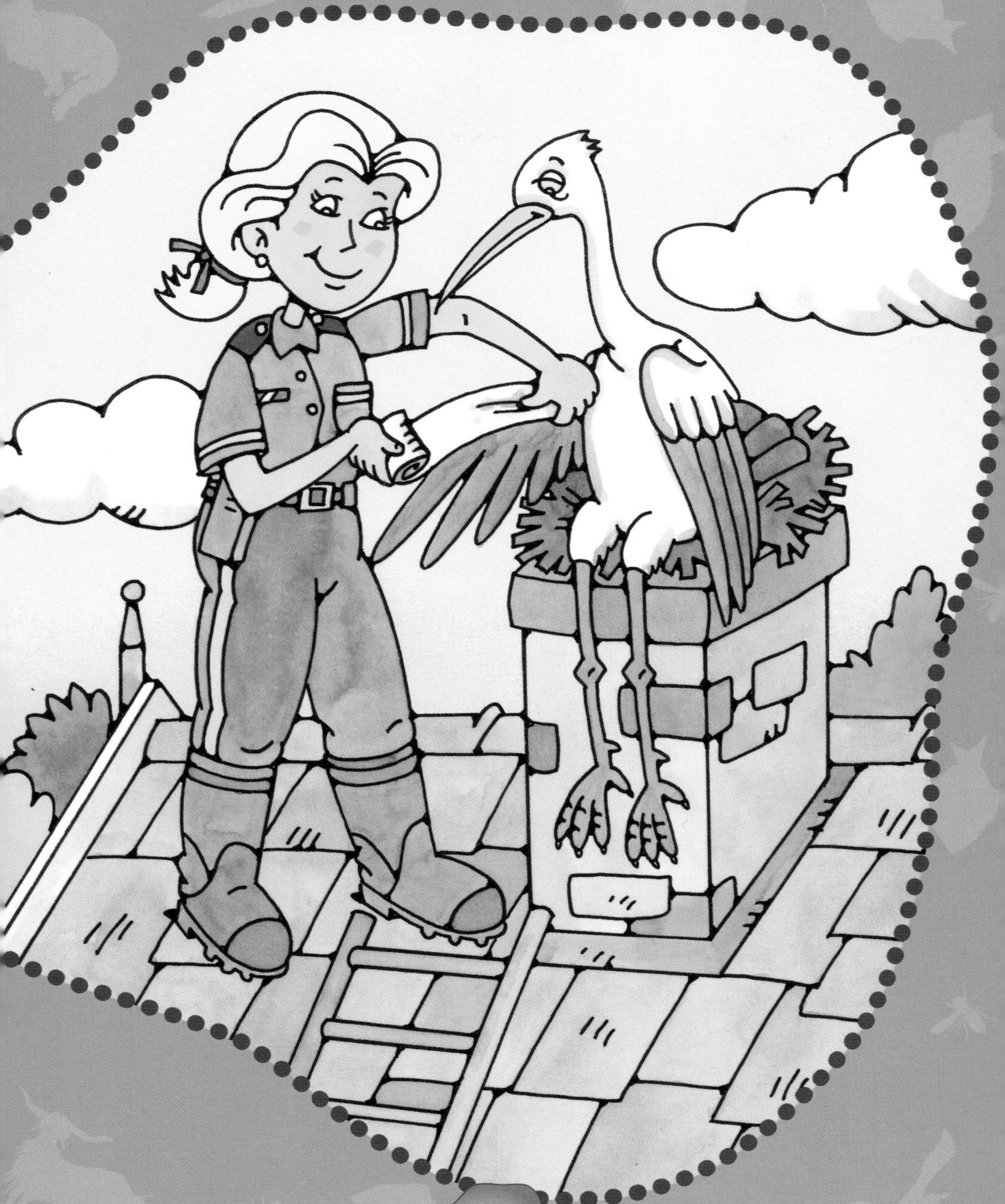

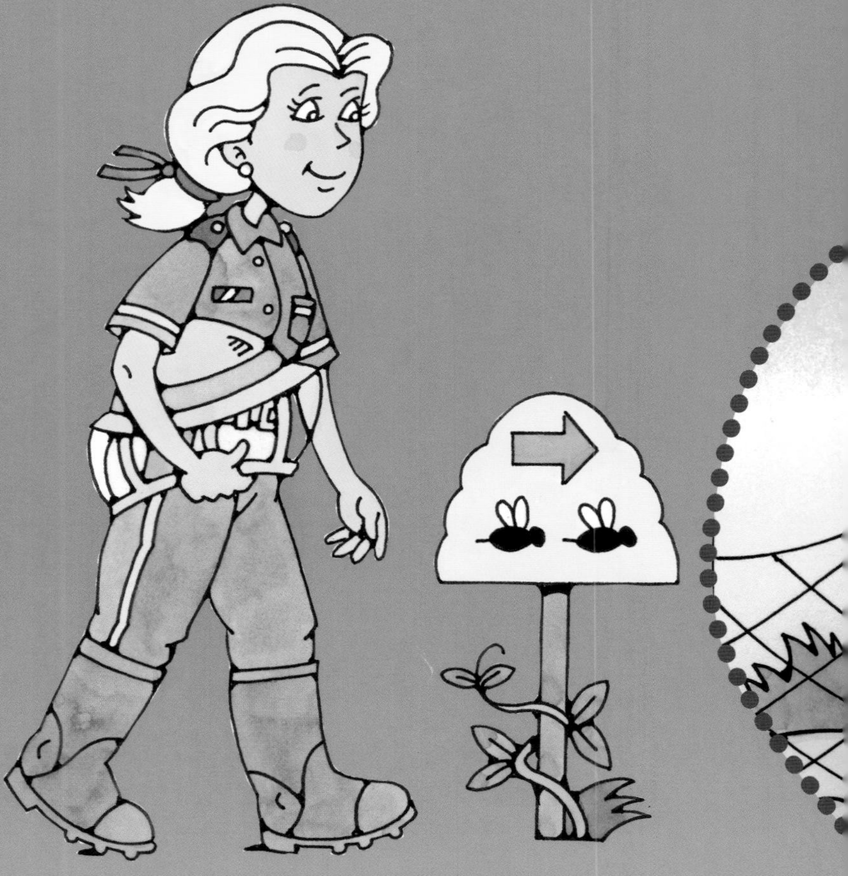

I can get the bees.

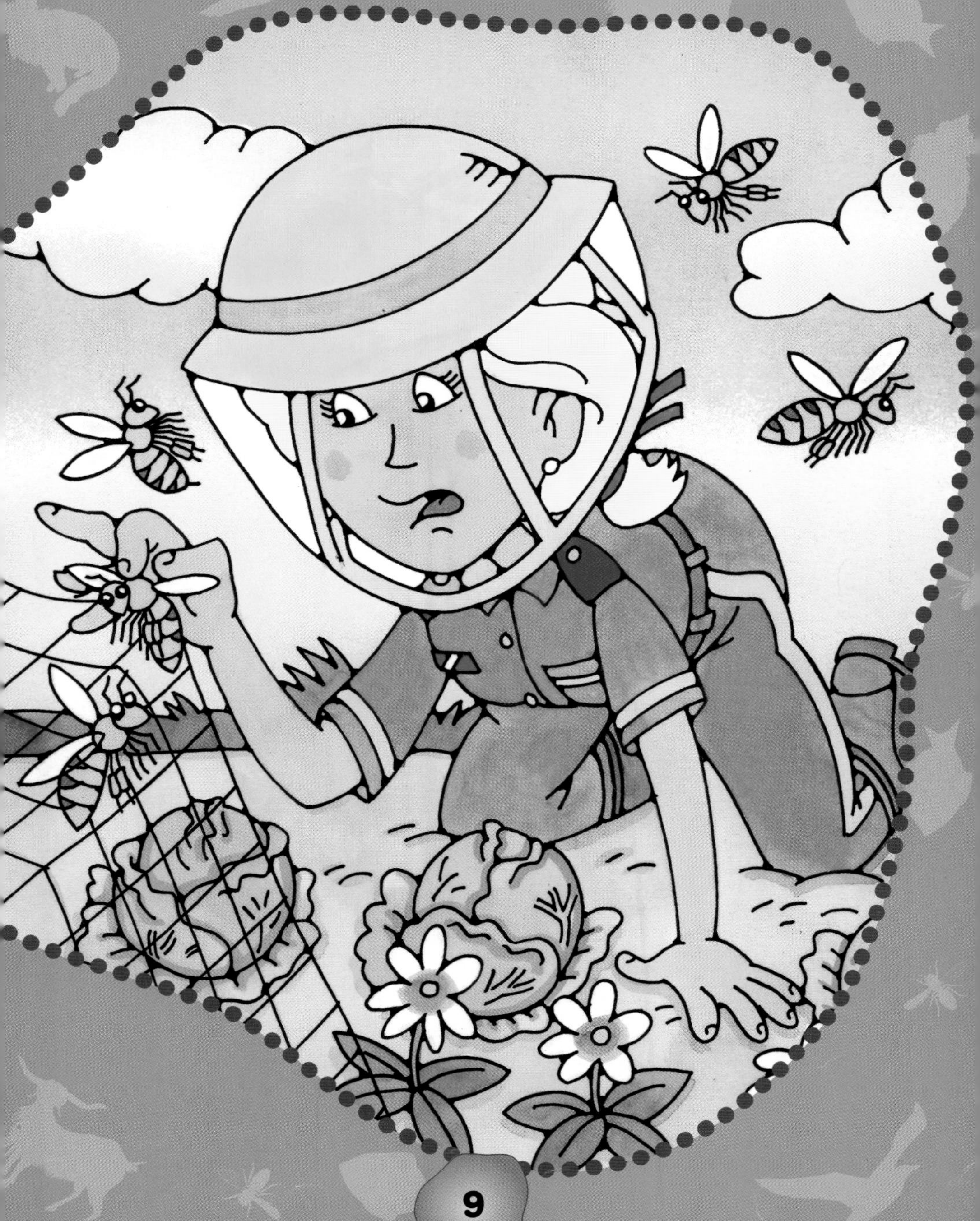

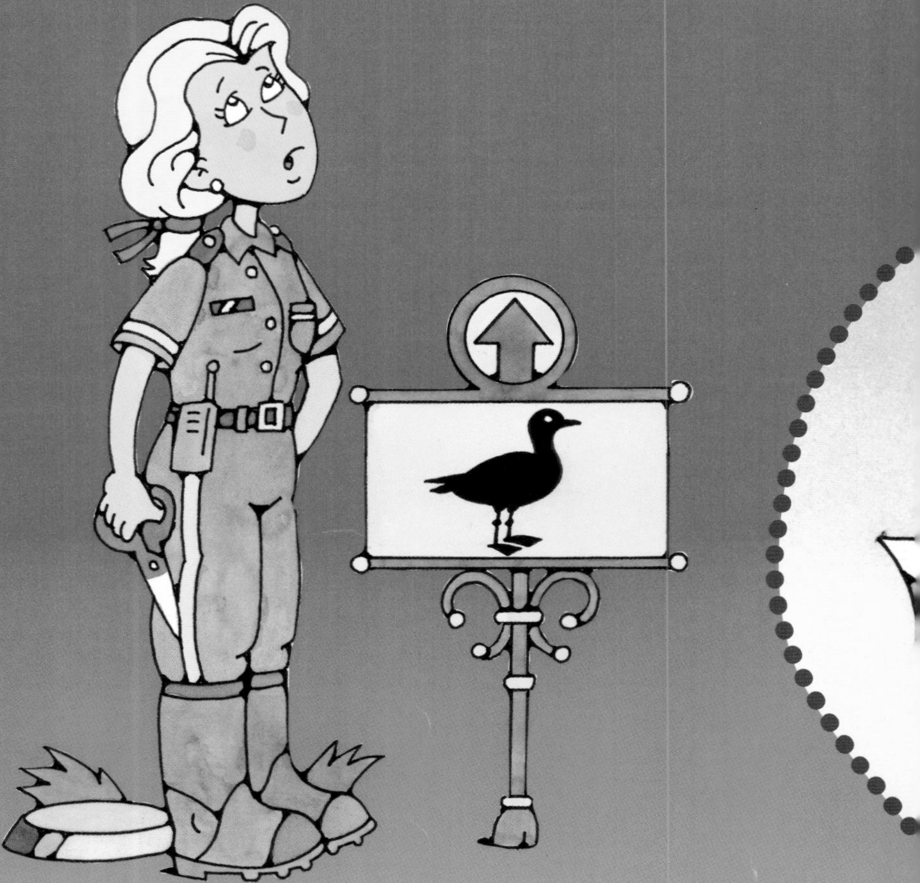

I can get the seagull.

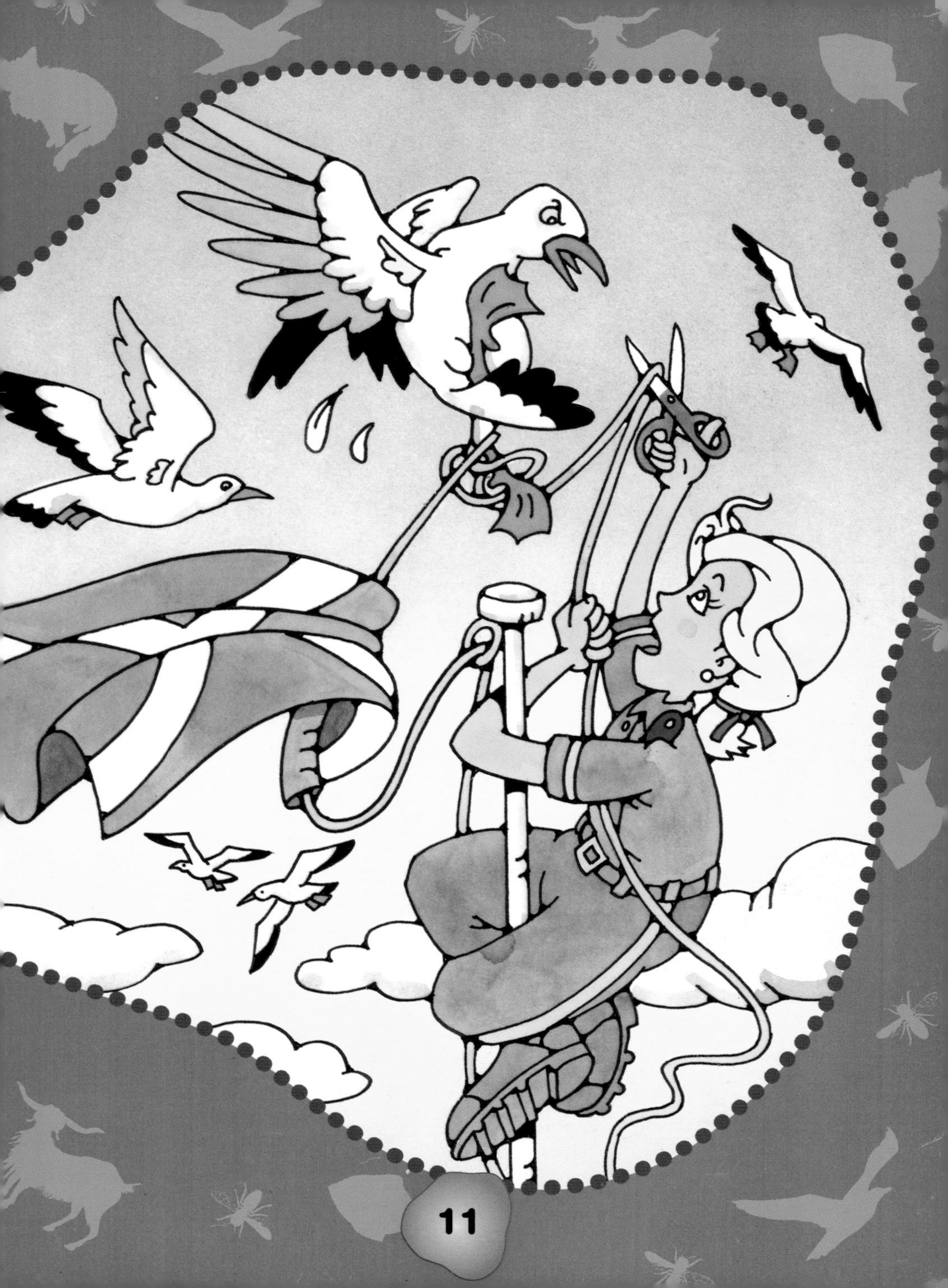

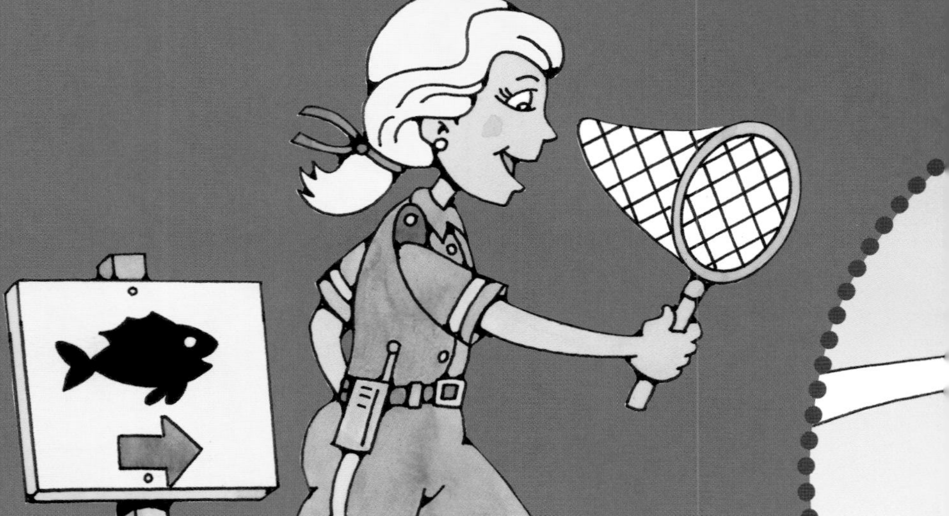

I can get the fish.

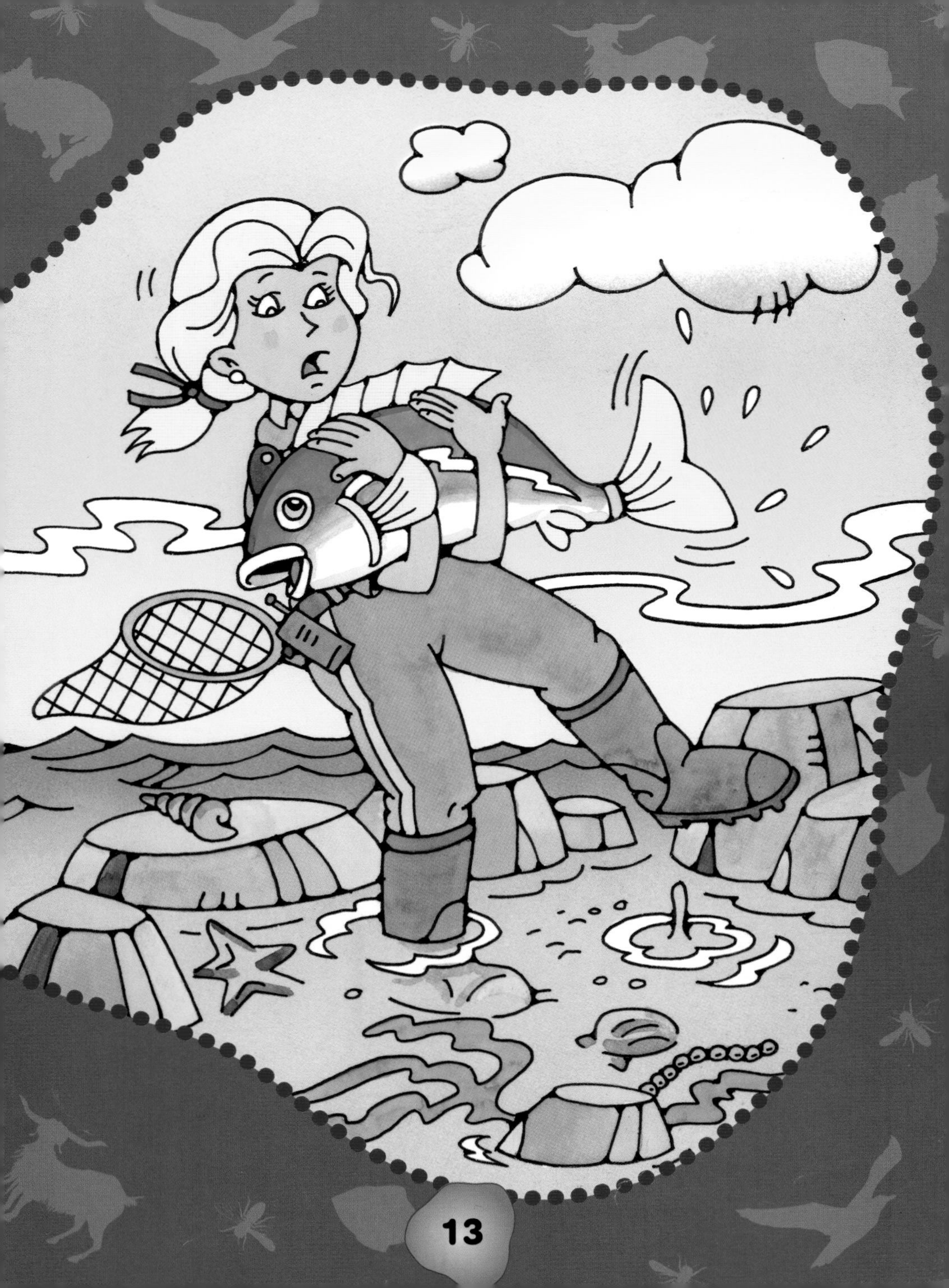

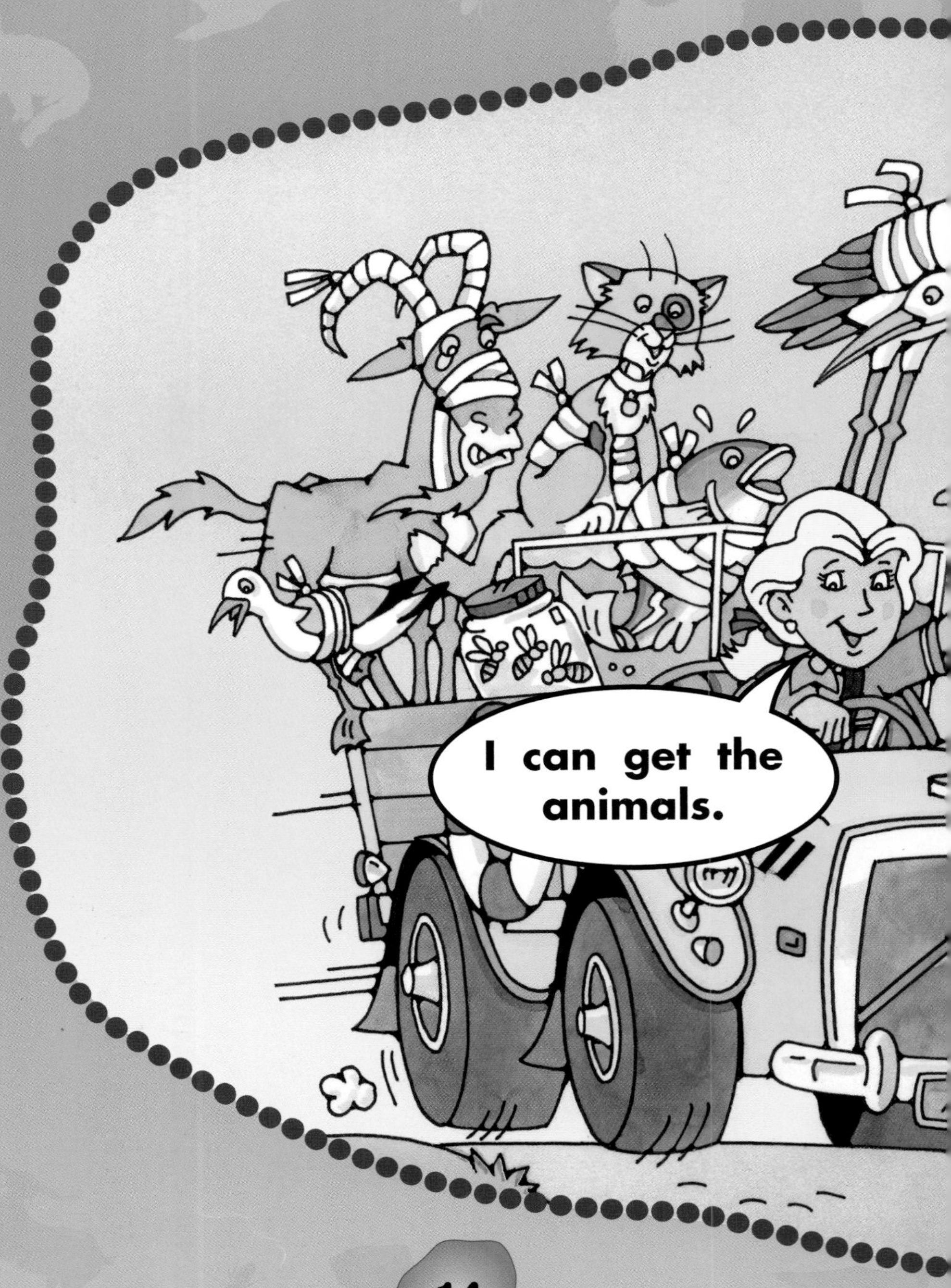
I can get the animals.

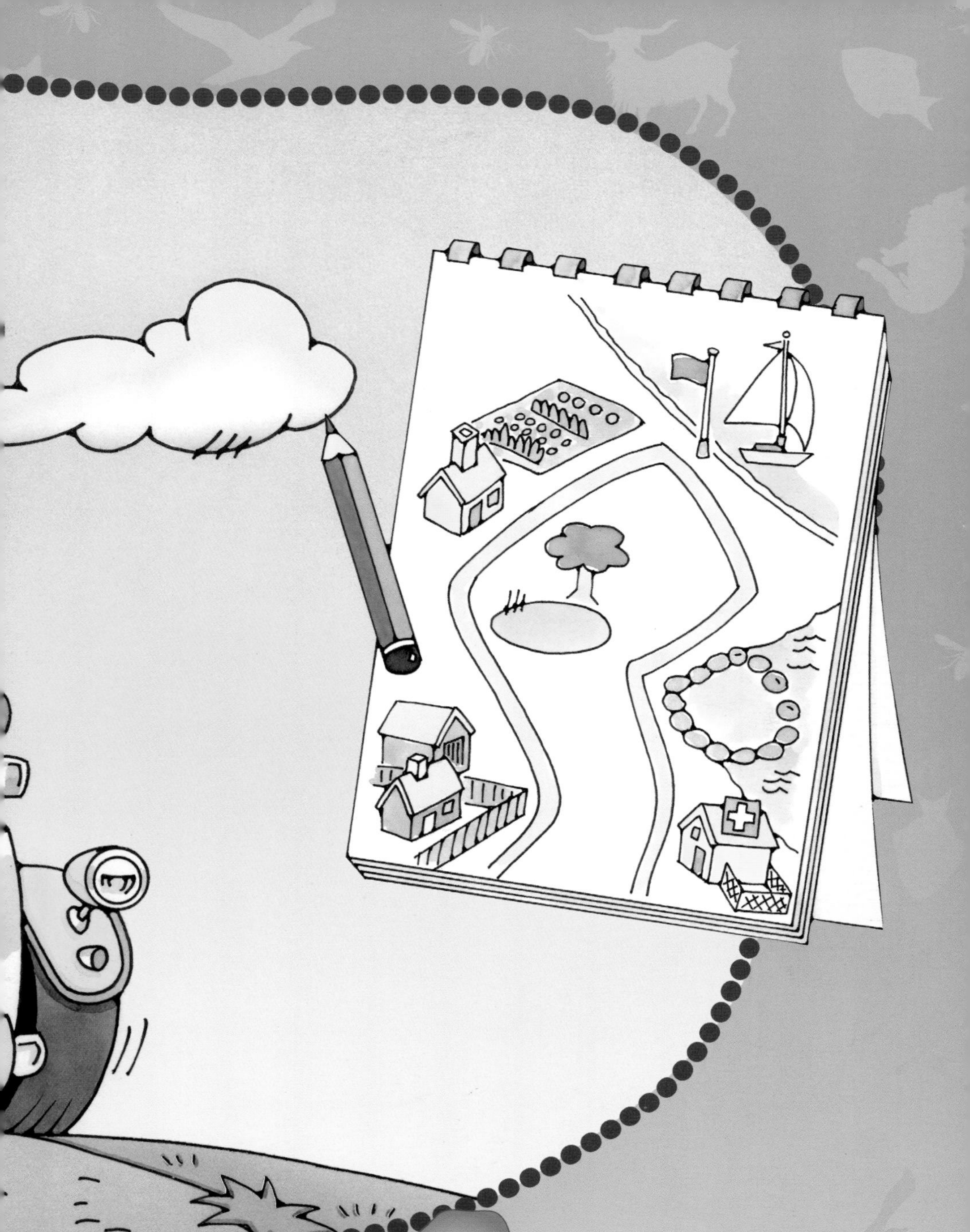

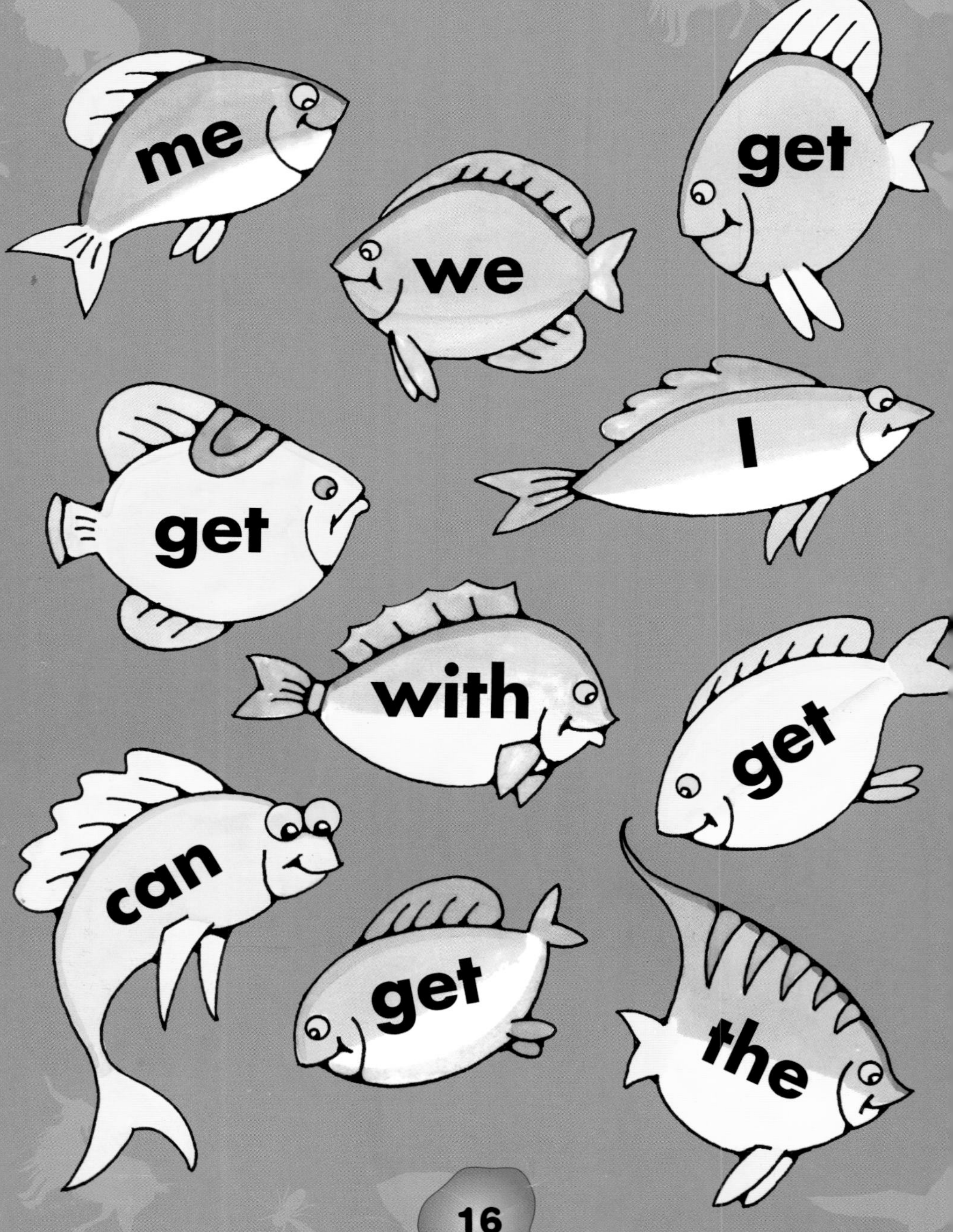
me
get
we
get
I
with
get
can
get
the